# No
# Messages

# THE ERNEST SANDEEN PRIZE IN POETRY

EDITOR
John Matthias

2001, *No Messages*, Robert Hahn
1999, *The Green Tuxedo*, Janet Holmes
1997, *True North*, Stephanie Strickland

# No
# Messages

Robert Hahn

UNIVERSITY OF NOTRE DAME PRESS
Notre Dame, Indiana

Manufactured in the United States of America


*Grateful acknowledgment is made to periodicals in which these poems
have appeared:*

*The Georgia Review:* "Object in an Inventory"
*Notre Dame Review,* "Epilogue and Unraveling"; "Escape from the
        Orkneys"; "Just One Look"; "No Place Like Home"
*Ontario Review:* "In the Open"; "John Ford on His Death Bed"
*The Paris Review:* "*Becalmed,* the Director's Cut"
*Partisan Review:* "The Flayed Man at the Fin de Siècle"
*Shenandoah:* "Do You Want to Talk About It?"
*Southwest Review:* "A Date with Sunset"
*The Yale Review:* "Yes"


*Library of Congress Cataloging-in-Publication Data*
Hahn, Robert, 1938–
No messages / Robert Hahn.
p.   cm. — (Ernest Sandeen prize in poetry)
ISBN 0-268-03652-7 (cloth : alk. paper) —
ISBN 0-268-03653-5 (pbk. : alk. paper)
I. Title.   II. Series.
PS3558.A3236 N6 2001
811'.54—dc21
                        00-056766

To

*Charles Alexander and Sarah Rachel*

and

*Berniece Mourer Hahn*

# Contents

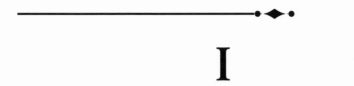

I

# Hail and Farewell at St. Andrews

## 1.

Over the ruffled patch of sand
Where castle and seawall meet,
A crow hangs in the wind,

Its steady gaze fixed on the shore,
Its eye clear.
I hail it as a messenger.

As if a last conversation
Were possible, and could still happen
Here at the world's end

Where John Knox was dragged from his pulpit
Down to a French ship.
Although I was never forced to believe

In anything of the sort,
Who wouldn't thrill to a herald
With news of the other shore?

Although the crow will lift away,
Its wings absorbed
In blank sky,

A dialogue dissolved, at last,
Or as usual, like a flake of floating ash,
Like a wafer on the tongue.

2.

After two years in a French galley,
Released but beyond recovery,
Knox believed words were literal still.

*Body of Christ, Blood of Christ.*
Asked to believe in "Divine Mind"
I grew up answering "nothing."

Had I been Catholic
I would have loved Communion,
It seemed so concrete,

The kneeling, the parting lips,
The solid sounds, so unlike
My inheritance from you, the keys

To a vaporous, unseeable realm
Where *error* and *air* were the same word,
Where details dissolved.

3.

Like Freud, your attendants
Had misread *Lear*.
"Wisdom," he said, "appears

Disguised in myth, asking the King
To renounce love and be friends
With the need to die."

The volunteers
Insisted on "talking about it"
And closed the door

On your final speech,
Delivered off-stage
And out of my hearing, lost

In particles of dust
With their own unfolding lives to lead,
In folds of the fluted curtains.

4.

If I knew
What you said and declaimed it,
Who would hear?

The crow with its wings spread wide
Makes a claim for meaning greater
Than anything I could say,

Now that one says so little, unless disguised
As molecular comedy, to hide
Its oracular origins.

5.

Gilt letters on a white wall declared
CHRIST'S THREE DAYS' WORK IN THE SEPULCHRE
PROVED DEATH UNREAL AND LIFE ETERNAL.

Who wouldn't save the best for last?
A cloud of sorcerer's dust
And the children who were locked in the attic

Are released, spirited away in a trunk
To tumble out later flushed and happy
As winners on *Wheel of Fortune*.

6.

Is anyone there
To welcome the stranger and say hello?
No band, no banner, no boat, no shore?

"Four times a year, we scatter the ashes from a plane"
Over the Superstition Mountains
Which as you never wearied of saying

Were purple at dawn, and deep blue at dusk,
And still are. Sometime therefore TBA
You will have joined the currents of dust

Rising on airstreams from the desert floor
To sway among the coral leaves
Of the stone flora.

7.

One could say the hovering crow
Was a stone figure, its arm raised
In wordless farewell.

Or a messenger no one heard.
Though Lester Young would say
If one person

Is really listening and even if he
Just went to the men's room
You have an audience,

Hearing words in their slow decay
From believing *body* and *blood*
Were transparent gates

To a world which is all
That is the case:
The seawall's

Pebbled concrete
And the castle wall's granite blocks
Framing the scene:

Yellow beach grass bending in the wind,
The blown sand,
The pale drained van Goyen light.

8.

The shapely, gestural clouds, the gulls
Wheeling down, the rooflines,
The walls, the narrow lanes—

There is another shore, facing
Our own, solid and detailed,
Where people like us

Go about their daily tasks.
Van Goyen's method
Was to plant himself on the sand,

His sea-level observation post,
And present the other world
Close at hand, unfolding in scenes

Whose radiance has been dissolved,
Where only the signature sepia light
Remains, for his plain demonstration.

# Canal and Camelback Mountain

But I know too
    that under the glassy skin
        is a function, no more to be denied

than the long decline
    of a steel mill, used as a set
        for post-apocalypse action films, I know

it is fed by pipes with
    plundered waters
        under the command of its authority

and you know all there is to know
    about this water, where it comes from, what it
        costs and the pros and cons

of alternatives but
    it is all
        pillage,

this system red in tooth and claw
    which works as well as anything else,
        we know its history

and tributes, Mussolini's
    muscular pillars,
        Futurist arcs and rays,

the scrubbed planes
    of Sheeler's industrial landscapes
        and Roebling's elegant answer

to the art of suspension
  hovering over the Ohio
    in the mirrored sunset.

At this hour
  the canal is all artifice,
    released from obedience

to be pure image, obsidian stele
  or white marble street in Corinth
    where thoroughbred races were run

to honor the dead
  colors streaming by as the jockeys
    bend to their tasks

as the colors plunge to a
  drained reversal, pure and precious
    as an inky Whistler nocturne or these

recycled words
  offered to the dead for their
    nightly stroll beside still water,

words like the bleached clothes
  whose newness and freshness
    amazes them so.

At such times the canal has not
  forgotten its role
    it is only off duty

snaking with coppery
    green and orchid-orange
        until it flames out

and one can say then
    the mountain's craggy profile
        broods like a classical figure

of betrayal and grief
    or one who feels this
        could say it

as the great night turns and day
    returns to the desert where water flows
        down from the mountains

to the cities where we live today as you
    might expect
        respectful of authority.

# Say You Will

According to legend
 The ripple of a butterfly's wing
From one flower to the next, like a seducer
 Gliding among the guests,

Is the faintest of flutters here
 But halfway around the globe it tosses
Cars in the air
 And uproots trees, or actors

Gape at a wall as if it were so
 Which is all the same to us, later on,
Shaken like a leaf
 By a moment of true feeling,

The extra beats in your wrist
 Speeding up the breath
Of someone who answers, *why yes*, as if to say
 Anything is possible today,

It seems, and a door opens
 Where you saw no door although
It was there, you needed
 Someone to say so.

# Just One Look

*O toi, qui vois la honte où je suis descendue,*
*Implacable Vénus, suis-je assez confondue?*


Ye wrathful gods! What did you have in mind, to buy the picture
    Without seeing what it was? Just one look and you brought it home
        To fill a white space on the kitchen door, who knows why.
    I think it might have reminded you of Ghiberti's doors of paradise,
Somehow, the dazzling scenes in this silver-and-black exhibit poster

Whose rhythm is vaguely familiar, whose rows of panels are artful enough,
    No longer the sardine cans they were but transformed, *objets trouvés*
        Bathed and polished to a lustrous glint, their lids
    Peeled away, and elliptical scenes within, hammered in low relief,
*Cloisonner*-small, each surrounded by a backdrop of midnight plush,

A blackness that swarms and gapes, like deep suicidal pauses in Chekhov,
    Like the blank gaps in the Parthenon frieze, which centuries later
        It seems we have not seen clearly—those figures we assumed
    Were wending their way to a feast, the usual grist for a poet's mill,
Are a deadly processional, on their way to a human sacrifice, and the daughter

Whose rounded hips sway beneath her pleated gown has another story.
    She is doomed. What we took for serenest art is a mad scene, a plea
        To those implacable gods who withdraw themselves at will,
    Whose random returns invade us, in forms we can hardly face
In the mirrors of our darkened rooms. They rise within us

And float back down, and now what we took for surface is not,
    And the thin layer of sea, which you saw from the plane window
        As the aquamarine of a travel poster, is something else,
    A refracting realm where you sink confounded, descending in reefs
Unfolding their umber feathers, and the shadows in fact are caves,

The hiding places of blue flashes and orange gleams and eyes looking up.
　　　How strange you must appear to them, in their trembling sky,
　　　　　With luminous beads of air trailing behind you.
　　　How strange you were in those afternoons of greenish light
Drained through the curtains, bizarre, as he curled tightly behind you

In echoing curve where you kneeled and raised your hips,
　　　How deep that was you murmured in the pillow as you pressed
　　　　　Your face down in a pose of devotion, and how absurd,
　　　How indecipherable those images were, as you pleaded,
As you looked back and lifted your head, to kiss, in tribute

To the visitation you would later call delirium, those afternoons
　　　No longer you, denied, or half-forgotten, like Ghiberti's doors
　　　　　Which burned in your sight the day you first saw them,
　　　The low swell of their sinewy metal, the flaring bronze
Of scenes you had known from black-and-white photos mounted on boards,

Pored over in a library carrel, barely remembered, like the vertigo
　　　When you reached the top of the tower and looked down,
　　　　　The unwilled *Oh* as the roofs and squares below
　　　Swarmed in new shapes, drifting back down again, and sifting away
Until one day, who knows why, you kneel in surprise before the door

To see these almost abstract patterns like stylized flora and fruit,
　　　These fragments of scenes, for what they are: a shoulder, a thigh,
　　　　　A tongue flickering in a wreathed grotto, an ardent arbor,
　　　A rising stalk in the grip of a guiding hand, a finger crooked
As it probes a ripe fig, a rondure tipped in glittering arousal,

Steamy variations pleased, as you see, by repetition, silvered scenes
    Of swooning Eros, afloat in a setting of sheerest black,
        Which is not the design element we thought, but night
    Falling on our *fêtes galantes*, on the torchlight and lutes,
On the small glowing scenes drifting in the dark, from which our gaze

Is averted. There is no limit to the power of our denials
    And the forms we give them, the rows of columns glinting
        In the sun, the measures of the temple whose inner steps
    Lead down to the spring, which is so cold your forehead aches
When you cup your hands and lift its shadowed water to your face.

# The Flayed Man at the Fin de Siècle

"Not to enchant" was the new prescription,
Not to bemuse or charm, but to witness,

And so restore the power art once had,
To transform and to save. But when was that?

And who were these new masters, who prescribed
The right poses, as if one could be right

About suffering? Consider the case
Of the Flayed Man, his face sculpted by pain

Indescribably, though it's Mannerist,
His lips contorted into waves which twist

Around a hollow mouth, from which a scream
Pours forth, to drain meaning of its meaning

Once and for all. The procedure begins
When a crank is turned, and the strip of skin

A surgeon has prepared is ripped, and rolled
Up on a spit. It ends by unfolding

A map of new, red flesh. "What kind of times
Are these?" *Man Being Flayed*, 1590,

Renders in paint a public spectacle
Which for centuries was nothing special

Though it had a purpose. When Romans lined
A brick road with men they had crucified

The point of that anguish was to be plain,
Less cruelty than communication.

But when a pious Japanese surgeon
Tries vivisection, only to observe

The effects, times have changed. "The man was strapped
Down on a bed. He seemed resigned to what

Was happening—but then when I began
To cut the chest open, from the top down,

I'd never seen a face like that, heard sounds
Like that, such howling, come from someone's mouth"—

A text not taken from a war-crimes trial,
But the good doctor's log—"after a while

It stopped." The time was 1942,
A prison camp whose horrors could outdo

Belsen, with new experiments each day.
For example, two men were stripped naked

In a courtyard. Inside, behind windows,
The officers could watch, and set down notes

As they observed the men begin to freeze,
Who knew how soon. Thirty below zero.

"Toward the end, their agony was so great,
They tore each other's flesh with fingernails."

I know nothing. To witness this outrage
Changed nothing for these men. No one was saved.

My only hope, my only prayer for them
Is that it end, that their agony end,

As it did, but not soon. Their murderers
Would live on, in a Tokyo suburb

Where they would treat patients and tend gardens
With painstaking care and die in their beds.

Time would pass. The long century would close
That began with Apollinaire's great "Zone,"

And ended, where, with "Flow Chart," or "Garbage,"
Amidst the canon wars, once all the rage.

Auschwitz and Hiroshima were the end
Of art, we said, as if they could have been.

# Guilt

They are waiting for you patiently
After their day at the beach

Their damp hair combed straight back
Their polished legs gorgeously tan

Dangling as they loll on the porch
In the canvas chairs like purple orchids.

They have been waiting for you to arrive
And lift your cherished, ceremonial knife

To carve the lemon peel
Slowly, as in a still life by de Heem,

So the artful coil will unwind
In gilt-encrusted light.

# Object in an Inventory

A sculpture of a sneaker
    in molded plastic of bright pink
        about the size

of a baby stroller
    mounted on wheels,
        an *objet trouvé*

so singular and unexplained
    one wonders why it exists at all
        let alone here

on the frozen margin of Plum Island
    (where of course I think of Elizabeth Bishop,
        watching sandpipers

rush back and forth along the edge
    of what appears to us
        as next to nothing)

where the ribbed, rock-hard sand
    scoured by a January wind
        is a natural trope for the mind

in its unfurnished state,
        richer now by this idea
                contained in a thing itself,

its past a mystery, its rolling days
        whatever they were
                all over now

a blank frame
        in the frieze of someone's memory,
                observed and recorded

one could say placed
        like an object in a box of Joseph Cornell's
                if many hadn't said so before

(a photograph of Joseph Cornell
        is found in an inset cabinet
                with glass doors

above my kitchen table, along with a photograph
        by James Merrill, and a white tile
                brushed with a blue pomegranate).

If Descartes decided, sitting by his stove
        in a small Bavarian farmhouse
                one winter

"one can find in oneself
        an infinity of ideas of certain things
                which cannot be assumed

to be pure nothingness"
　　　it is equally true that you find things
　　　　　where you happen to find them,

and though anyone might have seen the thing that day,
　　　it was you, and so
　　　　　it is yours, another form

in search of its function
　　　added to the mind's junk
　　　　　like Lefty Frizzell's version

of "The Long Black Veil"
　　　and its whining refrain, *nobody knows and nobody sees*
　　　　　*but me*

and the epic poems of Robinson Jeffers read straight through
　　　one winter week of your freshman year
　　　　　at Oberlin College, never returned to,

and Berlioz's *Faust*
　　　on a black breathless August night
　　　　　high in the half-empty amphitheater

at Epidaurus, hardly the place you expect to find
　　　the Paris Opera and Faust
　　　　　making his red-lit descent

into Peloponnesian stone
while the clamor rose above him,
the washed up relic

of somebody's bright idea
added to the trove of bric-a-brac
whose sense awaits disclosure.

# How Long Has This Been Going On

If, when the blue heron rises on the deeply waving strokes
Of its wings, and glides from one side of the pond to the other,
The moment is over too soon, it is slow enough, for us,
If nothing like Time in the life of the pond, abandoned here

When a glacier withdrew at last to its vast northern silence.
You could see the pond, sunk in its fold of dunes, from the ridge
Where cliff swallows crisscross the path at your feet, if you looked down
Past the quivering, balancing terns, and you could see us

On the beach below, as we were when Laura abruptly arrived,
Distraught as Isabelle Adjani in *The Story of Adele H.*
She called from England, and caught the next flight, away from her husband
And his "blonde bimbo," a ménage à trois doomed to be brief.

How could her marriage be over? The sun hung overhead,
Motionless, as she wrote her baffled, voluminous letters.
His answers were composed, her history revised. In the new ending,
The Prince would stay with his true love, and Maggie return to America.

We said good night and left her reading by a lamp on the porch.
The heron had settled down by then with its mate, a constant pair
Who came to the pond each summer, and sailed south in the fall,
Down the coastline, to Florida, until it was time to return.

The largos of their travels were long, if nothing compared with the cycles
When forests burn and the earth is covered in ash and ice
Which melts into seas, those vast eras which are, for us,
Overwhelming, like a childhood nightmare of an infinite task,

To lift the beach grain by grain to another shore.
We need a measure we can bear, although too soon completed,
Like the few hushed prolonged seconds when the heron rises
And glides to the other side of the pond, and floats back down.

# Do You Want to Talk About It?

If our genre scene, *The Lovers' Quarrel*,
Plays without words, it is because
We are perfect for the parts.

Our silence drifts out
Of the rented house,
Onto the deck, and into the airless evening.

Threads of black cloud
Brush over the lights on Indian Neck
But nothing stirs. Not a sound

From our new neighbors down
Where the French Canadians were.
I miss them already,

Their wordless tunes in the outdoor shower
Shah boom shah boom, yah dah da da,
Their bare feet drumming on the porch

As they turned the corner and went inside.
Shouldn't we invite some friends to visit,
Doris whose job is so boring

Who can understand it or Raymond
Whose roman à clef stays locked forever?
But hang it all, let that Marlowe talk!

It spares us the tropical torpor
My parents warned me about.
Too much brooding

Will collect around you, they said,
Like darkness behind the stairwell
In Sargent's *The Daughters of Edward Boit,*

Those brilliant girls in the foreground
Who know all about the dark interior
And do not care. When the eldest daughter

Steps forward to speak
Her delivery is natural, her voice low,
And she takes such pleasure

In her story—which isn't new, of course,
But is enough. How well she tells it.
How easy it is to fall in love.

# Escape from the Orkneys

The sea is slate gray,
The air is peat-smoke and mist.
The stones are called the Standing Stones

The Blue Guide tells us, as if
That would help, but no one has a clue
What the stones meant

Or who the Picts were
Or what they splashed on the walls
To appease the gods. What was Pictish at all,

For that matter. I think
These stones are like works
Of the Late Modern age, gray on gray,

Or white on white,
Luminous rectangles hopefully arranged,
Blank fields hovering on the edge of sense.

They are like the abstract paintings
I found in an underground mall, in Albany, New York,
Commissioned by Nelson Rockefeller,

Grim in their subterranean gloom, beneath an avenue
Where the giant tilted cubes and arcs of a modern
Imperial city rose, and so on, but to resume,

The Stones are arranged in a wide ring
At intervals that might have meant something,
At certain hours, depending on the sun and moon.

So we set up our tripods, and the cameras
Whose whirrs are a comfort to us. Standing Stones.
Cutaway views of the round mound houses.

Stone bed and hearth. Stone barn. Stone byre.
DRY STONE WALLS, CHEAP AND RELIABLE
Says a hand-lettered sign by the roadside.

The same stone. The same walls.
We are back in the Stone Age
With little or nothing to distract

From *silence et prière*,
No local color, no highlights
Glancing in the polished curves

Of a black sedan
Whose passengers pour from the doors
And flow up the stairs like a chorus,

No boulevardiers under domed umbrellas
Where the gaslit cobbles swim with color,
No trolley grinding around the corner

With figures riding by, whose stories
We know, on the stiff wicker benches
Lacquered a bright lemon yellow.

# Paradise Mall

What more could I do? While you were sleeping,
Who knew for how long, I went out to kill
Some time. The pavement wavered in the desert heat.
How cool it was in the Paradise Valley Mall

Where throngs of afternoon shoppers wove their way
Through the aisles and rising tiers, where lush
Palm trees rose to the pitch of a glass canopy
And the tall curtain fountain fell with a hush

To the floor. In the flowing crowd, I felt no more
Or less surreal than anything else that day,
Where striped umbrellas shaded the tables below
At The Coffee Connection, like or unlike the café

At Chartres, beside the cathedral, in a view
From the top of the tower. When you turn to look back down,
The world unfolds, the orange and red tiled roofs
And the patchwork of spreading fields, in pasture or plowed,

The squares of green and tan anticipating
Cézanne and the cubists, as if a long century
Was still to come and its solid, logical landscape
Would still be there, if you could wake from your sleep.

# Yes

*When someone stops eating*
   *It's the body's way*
*Of saying it's time to leave*
   We hear the volunteer say

But how hard it is to stop hearing
   In the shell when you press
Its hollow to your ear
   These echoes of please and yes

More sound than words
   When meaning lets go,
A low moan, or deep sigh, heard
   As overtones

Of *please*
   Of *yes*
Who long to persist in our being
   On a narrow ledge.

# *Picnic* Suite

1. *Langue et Parole*

"You are so *beautiful*," they told Kim Novak in *Picnic*,
But she was tired of words that were all palaver

And meant one thing. She saw right through
The lingo of guys who only wanted to lay a hand

On her arbor of overripeness, her *pêches d'été*.
What she wanted was a cadence of light on water

Or the greenish glow in a long avenue of oaks
After rain, oh, but it sounded worn out and sonorous

Already. Lovely words. Not that hers were better.
Real tough talk came natural to her—

She knew about football and poker and beer,
She knew rock and roll, and the down-home sound

Of fists on flesh, and the hard words you need
To describe a small town and a narrow street

And her plain house. She sat on its screened-in porch,
She lived there, remember? She wanted out.

She was like a painter who returns to the same river
Over and over, adrift in its faintest variations

As if such journeys would take her somewhere
She hadn't been, where presence was possible.

As if to *long* for the sublime could be enough.
What did she want? Who knew. She knew how much.

2. "Moonglow"

A new version of the old song
        Kim Novak and William Holden
                Danced their slow dance to in *Picnic*

Forty years before. The brushes circle
        On the shadowed snare
                And the strings release the notes

All over again, like ripples from stones
        Dropped in a pool.
                I should have known

Her numinous arms, his
        Rolling hips,
                Those cloudlike god-sized

Figures of pink and peach
        Floating overhead were emblems
                Of pure possibility

Only to me. What they saw in each other
        Was darkness
                Flowing into darkness

And finding its familiar shape.
        He was a roustabout,
                She was the best-looking girl in town.

Nothing would change about that
    And when they talked their words
        Affirmed it. It was too bad.

What they wanted was less transparent
    More flared and crazed with glazing
        Layers, like Mallarmé,

But they didn't know words like that
    So they opened their arms
        And danced

Until their two
    Forms were a single Romance
        Backlit by the moon.

3. Lamoille River Seduction

One summer evening as I crossed the bridge
  And turned along the river's edge

As a gull wheeled over the pines
  And a sliver of moon rose

A trio of round sumptuous sounds
  *Moon, gull, Lamoille*

Chimed in with the sonorous promise
  One tries so hard to resist.

Was I not warned, did I not learn, this
  Is the betrayer who leaves us

Seduced and abandoned
  In the small towns we longed to escape?

The day we lifted our glasses at Vernon
  While the Seine went on to Giverny

With its sluicegates and reflecting pond
  And engineered views, I recalled,

As if on cue, a line of lugubrious song
  *When I dream about   the moonlight   on the Wabash*

*Then I long for   my    Ind i a na     home*
    Which did no more for the unseen Wabash

Awash in the suicidal debris
    Of Ross Lockridge and James Whitcomb Riley

Than all these gulled and beguiled words in their rise
    And fall can do for the foul Lamoille.

## 4. A Southern Indiana Boyhood

There is no excuse for this indulgence, unless
The delusion of returning to a new source
In old material, these "rolling hills"
In the car window's glancing version
Of late winter landscape

And this cross-hatching of spindly trees
Recalled in Corot-like spangle and arch
Over blacktop roads, where steam that rose after rain
Hung in white veils like an epiphyte,
The fretwork of a bridge, a flash of green water

And a bank where nude figures lolled
In a scene by Bouguereau, and there you are,
Back home again, in words wending there
Like sonorous colors pulled from the cello.
The figure you saw at Avignon, on the other shore,

Was the one you left, waiting for you
To return, the same old you, so dull it is better
If we don't speak at all, as in those days
We swayed to avoid each other when we passed
Like cartoon ghosts in our long hall,

Not a word between us, not a sound, even music
Could be read as a flag of truce to break the silence,
Our new esthetic, whose white space spread
Like sky over sages on a cliff.
If we say nothing we are not betrayed.

Or say no more than two or three words
Like round white stones
Dropped in a pool.
Or placed in the furrowed sand of the Garden of Repose.
If we leave a _____, or a pause

More can be assumed, and the reader can be beguiled
By a late-breaking illumination
From our travels, something understood
When anything could still be learned, when we drifted
In a sea of feeling, where everything was possible.

5. Some Pigs

Dark green pines
       In a sculptural cluster rising
              On your right

Balanced by a field of easily flooding light
       On your left: this is the mass and expanse
              Of classic landscape painting

As Kenneth Clark explains, a famous order.
       But it is all abruptly trashed
              When you reach the next farm,

A Richard Scarry children's scene where pigs run
       Loose with cows and outbuildings are half-collapsed
              And rusting hulks are enjambed

With new, bright green tractors, a disjunction
       So extreme it could reflect
              An esthetic,

The world left in a natural state
       Whether newborn or moldering or abandoned,
              Let be,

Not sprayed or veiled or bejeweled
       Like rinds and seeds in a still life by de Hooch
              But the true *pays*,

True presence, where all is compacted and shit
       And slime pile up and smell so badly
              My friend Judy who writes about myth

In her house farther down the road
    Hates to drive by it, hates above all
        The foul unfathomable barn

Whose long side opens like the fourth wall of a stage
    Disclosing back in its dark recesses
        The wretched vealers

Lying near a stack of hides.
    I don't blame her. This is
        The primal place

We need to return to, not childhood but back
    Before we knew how to say *moon*
        Before we knew names

Like *Bill* and *Kim*
    To drop in the ear
        Like pebbles in a trembling pool.

This is the place to breathe deeply of
    Where our longings and ardent language dissolve,
        A wile

To escape the toils of Beauty, whose fleshy arms
    Ringed with bracelets
        Beckon, where she turns on her throne

And calls us, in her murmuring, purling voice
    Whose cadenced chants
        Restore us to swine.

# Sentimental Journey

JOCKEY TONY DESPIRITO DEAD AT THIRTY-NINE

The cover of *Time* at sixteen—so young,
So famous, the announcer called his name
At a close finish, not *Lucky Lady*
Or *Poet's Alchemist*, but *look here comes*

*Tony Des-par-eeto on the outside*
*Flying like the wind!* Such fame had its cost,
Of course. He had the last rites twice and lost
A spleen and kidney, but came back each time,

Reborn while he was up and streaming by
In his colors. The Kid! An immortal,
If doomed to fade away like Delmore Schwartz
And Ridgely Torrence, whose vague company

He joined at last, living with the Unknowns
Somewhere in Rhode Island. Until today,
Flying like the wind I am pleased to say,
He crossed to the inside, and brought it home.

# No Messages

He woke at 3:00 A.M. from a dead sleep. Where was he?
Clearly it was not the grave of Mary Baker Eddy
With a telephone under its classical-revival dome
And a line in to Divine Mind, "proving Death unreal
And Life eternal." He was on his own,

In the dark. When the drowsy morgue attendant
Heard his pounding, the long drawer of stainless steel
Opened upon an amazing sight: a man not dead, not dead at all,
Only waking from a coma. And with this semi-miracle
The tale, if the ending was happy, would end.

But his fiancée was a true believer
Who listened to her elders. A man *who had been dead*,
They said, walking in their dusty lanes again, more sleepily
Than before, with a more distracted air, was *undead*.
A zombie! She canceled the wedding and refused to see him.

Was this a great turning aside?
Did she miss her chance with one of the lords of life,
To walk and talk with a true companion, a traveler
Who has seen across to the other shore?
I think she did. In other words, I think I did

When my father finally crossed, without a word,
Or nothing much. What did he have to say?
"Son, you would be amazed
The things I've learned about myself in here,"
Like a talk-show guest on the self-help circuit,

And "Rock and roll!" when the doctors announced
"Comfort, yes, but as for healing
Your own beliefs will be more help than we are, now,"
And we wheeled him out for a last drive home.
The setting there was familiar. Or so it seemed.

Dust and sunlight glazed the leaves of the palms.
Narrow shadows inched away from the stucco walls.
The day cooled down. In the morning by 6:00 A.M.
Runners already circled the pond, while geese and swans
Crossed its breathless mirror. None of this mattered to him.

Not even the difference we tried to conceal,
As in the tale of a soldier, captured on the eve of D day,
Who wakes from a drugged coma in a scene
That looks like home. It is a play
They have staged, and his role is to spill his secrets,

As he almost does, but! an overlooked sign
Betrays them, a word in the wrong language, a detail,
Like the oxygen tank in the corner, they have failed to hide.
The domed steel cylinder hooked to its coils
Of tubing might have seemed obvious, even if he did decline

To see it. The volunteers wanted to "talk about it," but why?
The tumors spreading thickly woven branches
In his lungs, densely printed with more bad news
Each day, were enough. When my mother called at last,
At 8:00 A.M. Eastern and 5:00 Arizona time,

Her prayer was answered, his terror was over,
The long nights in the dark room (near the phone,
To call his Christian Science "practitioner")
With nothing he wanted to read anymore,
Not even *Science and Health with Key to the Scriptures,*

And nothing on the fifty cable channels
He wanted to see, not now, not even *Jeopardy*
Or *Wheel of Fortune.* I saw him walking down the hall,
His bare feet shuffling on the cool, red tiles
As he flicked the trailing cord out of his way

And closed the door behind him. No last words.
*No Messages,* the Voice Mail voice reports, although
There are messages, of course, when you return
To the office, where you seem to move more slowly,
Like someone in a trance. You are not yourself, they observe,

You are like a figure from a horror movie, the Zombie,
Gliding down a hallway in the middle of the night.
The guests are all sleeping—or are they?
One of them wakes in a cold sweat as the steps go by
And a shadow crosses the narrow band of light.

# String of Beads

A row of water beads
    flows down the pane of the bay window
        where I listen

to the woman across the street
    who plays the piano every day as if
        nothing else mattered.

When the beads roll down the screen
    they are globes
        whose round gleamings

are perfect worlds, as they sink
    in vertical rows
        falling into place

with suspicious ease, like daughters
    arranging themselves by height
        eager to please.

Do we see the world better without these charms
    hung where the world should be?
        But the world is out there,

we wake up fearing it has gone away but no
    it is bored with us
        and our travels,

but is still there
    in the *Times* the rictus of a face
        twisted by hate, a pious Haredem

flinging rocks and shit
        at Jewish women who
                want to pray at his wall, but!

*no women*, no daughters, it is impure
        to hear
                the voice of a woman raised in song

YOU ARE NOT REAL JEWS
        he screams as he tries to break through
                the restraining line of soldiers but what is

a real Jew?
        Such fine distinctions
                outrage us, such hairline fractures

dividing the world and the words
        that move us toward it or away,
                the half-transparent beads tracing

the screen, and the notes struck from her strings
        floating in the brownstone canyon,
                our cameo world, like Chardin's

whose copper kettle and green glass vase
        have not forgotten their function,
                though idle now they still

recall in their prayers
        the Haitian whose head is shoved in the toilet
                the toilet plunger

shoved up his ass
　　the cops screaming their hatred
　　　　of the world, which is

out there whatever we say about it,
　　it is always there
　　　　behind the panel of repeating rows

collecting colors as the light deepens
　　into blue and gold streaks
　　　　like threads of a radiant shawl

stretched on its loom, through which one enters
　　as if through a wall
　　　　the life of the woman across the street

humming as she plays
　　a woman with whom
　　　　the gods are pleased

the gods who know it is all
　　practice
　　　　for what is still to be seen

the pure transparency to which we aspire
　　the screen of the waterfall
　　　　dissolved into sky

and the ways the world will call upon us,
　　the performance to come,
　　　　what is still to be done.

# II

# No One There

In Memoriam, James Merrill

*Art declares its caveat to the thesis according to which the time has come to
change the world. While art bears witness to the necessity of liberation, it
also testifies to its limits. What has been done cannot be undone; what has
passed cannot be recaptured.*

*. . . Inasmuch as art preserves, with the promise of happiness, the memory of
the goals that failed, it can enter the desperate struggle for changing the world.*

—Herbert Marcuse, *The Aesthetic Dimension*

*Mi chiederai tu, morto disadorno,
d'abbandonare questa disperata
passione di essere nel mondo?*

*(Will you ask me, unadorned dead man,
    to abandon this desperate
    passion to be in the world?)*

—Pier Paolo Pasolini, "The Ashes of Gramsci"

*If Su Shih saw this writing of mine, he would laugh at me,
for pretending to be the Buddha, when Buddha is absent.*

—comment by Huang T'ing-chien, on the
left-hand side of Su Shih's scroll, "Poems Written
at Huang-chou on the Cold Food Festival"

# Overture: The Bright Day

Weathermaps agree, it was a bright dawn
In the valleys of saying, or Tucson

At least. The sky's blank screen was crystal clear.
The scene was set. Within, a pearl Vermeer

Undertone welled up, and our savage star
Arose, on cue, to dazzling trumpet flares

Replayed all afternoon in blue gem-pools.
But at the sunset services, guess who

Was missing from the crowd. Shift to past tense.
What now? Should we try the parlor nonsense

Of Ouija board and cup? Are spirits still
On call? Spare us, please. That odd revel's spell

Goes back in its black hole. From Water Street
No cards from the Ideal Reader's sleeve

Will flutter down, no light across the Sound
Decode our message. "There's no one," as Pound

Complained when Henry James was gone, "to *ask*,"
Not that one would, the mirror blank at last.

Next scene TBA. Although Auden's line
"The words of a dead man are modified

In guts of the living" is not your style,
It gives one pause, if I'm the admirer

You have become. Let's say, you were a voice
Great within us but not the people's choice—

Who can blame them—so sumptuous, so far
From all that is the case, *Die Welt*, which art

Can't change—unless that is *precisely* why
One turns to Mozart, or Matisse, why time,

Having pardoned Kipling with this excuse,
Pardons you, for "eugenic solutions"

Heard from on high? Those deep-throated sources
Who took you backstage at *The Four Horsemen*

Wore comic masks, for distance, but closer
To home, around the coast from Sandover,

In Cold Spring Harbor, just a few years back
A real God-B in his genetic lab

Unveiled a model plan, to sterilize
A *long* list of "unfit," which caught the eye

Of Nazis, who came to call . . . Does this ring
A bell? No? Tell me, *what were you thinking*

To speak of "the great winnowing" as if
In your hushed rooms that theory's iron fist

Could do no harm? As if *a master race*
Was just a bright new thought whose mythy rays

Revolved in glass? Hello? You should have known
Better, although you were your father's son—

But enough. *Some* sons are born to "misread"
Pig-headed fathers, it seems, but believe

I am your faithful ravished fan, *enfin*,
If churlish, and doubtful. You're in good hands,

I think. Cold comfort, though? Your verses scroll,
Immortal, in this screen's cool lunar glow,

Scattered riches unfurled like a border
Of script, looping around an empty door.

# At the Northern Gate

When Horace calls, "Let the lamps burn,
Be private, and worry less—invite
The sweet-voiced Lyde to help us drink
    This Falernian wine,"

Let us drink, if rogues and scoundrels
Abuse the laws that keep them from harm
If the wretches in our care are no better off
    If small farms

Fail—and Quebec talks of secession!
A plan too bone-headed for words, surely—
Pour the Médoc, and let us hear
    Cecilia Bartoli

While we praise the curve of Lydia's calf
As if it were yesterday. This morning
When the sun came blazing into the mirror
    Like a messenger's torch

Before a cloud bank snuffed it out,
I thought, what if a mirror's memory
Could store and retrieve, for our instant recall,
    All it has seen . . .

"When we tilted the mirror, Alexandra and I
Could turn and see ourselves, wrapped
In a rapt embrace." Steven, thanks
    For sharing that,

A blossom fluttered from the floating world
Is precious tonight. The next phase
Looks dark. More of the same? The mind
        Receding in space

As it empties out our brushwork, our verses,
Our tales a thousand times revised
For the emperor, our affairs of state.
        *Govern wisely*

Said your card when I was appointed here.
I haven't been everyone's cup of tea
But so what—a judgment for the audience
        To make, or "history."

The card is a photograph from Mallorca
Where offstage sun throws a framework
Of shadows—a bird in its cage—over
        Your open notebook,

Its pages laced with graceful revisions
Of lines given by the gods. Is this
An image of Thought trapped in its plumage?
        So well hidden

One wonders—but what should poets do?
Must we rage, like the *Separatistes*
Whose aroused feelings are unviolated
        By the faintest idea

Of economics? In the T'ang dynasty
36 million were killed or left homeless
By An Lushan's revolt. The world
        Never leaves us alone

Even here in Tu Fu's retreat
(*That I am here, in a thatched hut*
*This flawless morning, gathers me in joy*).
        Come, fill the cup,

Let us recall a naked foot, a fall
Of hair, a bud reddened by a kiss,
Tiger orchids whose petals flare
        In the oblivious glass.

# Blocked Views, Bad Sightlines

We've been promised a glimpse of the *fleuve St. Lawrence*
But our window at the Westin
When its curtain-layers are whisked aside, flowered, then gauze,

Frames a drama of Capital Out of Control: high-rise
Neighbors whose hostile takeovers
Of one another's views reduce all lines of sight

To chaos. Modernist blocks and cubes vie with more recent
Fashions, inside-out pipes,
Rakish swerves of tinted glass, and the instant obsolescence

Of "post-modern" scallops and flutings. A bird's-eye view
Of a *fin de siècle*.
We've seen it. What's next? "I should be writing you

A proper letter," said your card, "but my eyes are full
Of floaters, and I need to spare them.
The next phase is shrouded in mist." Night falls,

Lights blink on, and steam rises from the towers like smoke
From Monet's locomotives
At the Gare Saint-Lazare—an image to give one hope

For a better day tomorrow, not entirely dashed:
Sunlight bounces off
A puzzle of smoked glass and steel, and spreads a lattice

Of shadow over the building *en face*, whose pale pink
Granite is veined with orange.
This found-object is brought to you by Poets, Inc.,

Specialists in the modern urban landscape since Apollinaire.
Mix reinforced concrete
With lightweight steel, and there it is, rising in the air,

The City. A universal language whose lines are fractured
Now, and decaying, like Art.
Theater for example. If to dialogue one adds a third actor

And basic stagecraft, in time Aeschylus and Sophocles
Are born, Lear and Phèdre
Suffer our sins, but *now* we have Neil Simon for comedy

And David Mamet for drama, okay in their way, but really
Where are we? Or where do we go
From here: the imploding maze of Language? Chaos Theory?

Astrophysics? The "poetry of science" already begins
To curve back wearily.
We can try Montreal's museum, with its fine Peter De Witte

Interior. Space makes sense in his wide room of tile,
Tapestry, and oak, opening
To rooms deeper within, each with a different tale

To tell (who's that in the alcove, watching a woman play
The clavier). The eye is led
Into reassuring, sensible recesses, layer by layer,

A trip back to the inner room through a sequence of stanzas.
But look, we almost missed
The *Landscape with a Man Pursued by a Serpent,* a late Poussin.

Order and balance rule. Nothing is crowded out.
The massed branches on the left,
The mysterious figure fleeing into the middle ground

Which yields to fields, hills, clouds whose round shapes
Echo the trees below.
Euclidean, but dreamlike. Well, if art *is* an escape,

This might do. It's worth a visit, to this oddly familiar
World, out of the question,
With a river curving toward us, a temple balanced on its hill.

# Raw or Cooked?

Banana peel on a green dumpster

           end of the line debris seen
                on a walk through North Beach

Coit Tower
with its school-of-Rivera murals

           bent backs of workers
      pig-eyed bosses with cigars, art

              with a purpose

The City Lights Bookstore

           where I heard
        Ferlinghetti
reading a line about his balls/"I am
      very attached to them," the hip crowd laughed

           in 1960/I was 22

If that was raw, you were high cuisine
      *Passé* debate?

        Snyder revived
          on a high mountainside

Ginsberg passed on
      from baddest boy to Buddhist saint, canonized,

all fading out

    across a millennium's blurring edge
             into new quarrels

but there were
      fighting words out here

when you stepped from the stagecoach with your
        embroidered valise

more my style
        than I like to admit
                too easily charmed, or dazzled

by Memling's deep gaze
        in the glowing pool
                of one emerald
                        set against velvet

        as if the world

as if I didn't hear this woman

                        crossing Columbus Avenue
                                in a wheelchair
slumped to one side
                        how could I miss her

I can see
        she is drooling I can hear
                        her bellowing
indecipherable words/speaking in tongues/her swollentongue
thick clots of sound wrenched from her throat

                    the closer she came
the more it was one word over and over, something like *hogwash*
                    hogwash hogwash hogwash

across the wide intersection
a messenger
                    rolling the word in my direction
                                in liberated verse.

# An Air Full of Ghosts

In the reading room window, a pearl gray
Wash of startled pigeons swirls
Across a scene from Richard Wilbur,
Clothesline strung between two pulleys

Where air is awash with flying costumes
Of earth-angels: pink tank tops,
Green underwear, blue socks—
Rainbow attire for a gamin troupe

Of tumblers—the acrobats of Crete,
The bull-dancers, your notion of a "heavenly"
Time-trip—but like Wilbur's elegant
Proof that this world is a clean

Orderly place, the fancy evades
The facts, the true-life tale of an urban
Mom with too many kids whose dirty
Laundry has just been reeled offstage.

Speaking of escapes, I'm off to meet
Anne and Steve at the St. Francis
Where the waiter still makes a fuss
About the right way to serve a martini,

Sweeping down on us with his tray
And its glass vial nestled in a bowl
Of crushed ice, a walk-on role
Which tall wall mirrors replay

While we feast on Washington's latest outrage,
Aghast, as if *we* knew what to do.
But face it, we have no solution,
Anymore than you, who didn't read the paper.

Is it true, does verse "that makes a virtue
Of exaggeration" fail the test
We expect of greatness, a "sane assessment
Of our most difficult cases"? Whew.

Maybe so, but some days I'd settle
For anything without a car chase.
Tonight we've tried, from euthanasia
To affirmative action, to prove our mettle

As thoughtful citizens and enough said
For one day. The merlot will wipe
Our slate blank tomorrow, and the mind
Resume its innocence. Time for bed.

—After breasting the tide of a Chinese
New Year parade, high school kids
Under waves of cloth and glitter.
Their dragons wind through the street

To banging drums and wailing flute,
Messengers from another world . . .
Last year, my father's ashes whirled
Away on the updraft, having been strewn

Over the Superstitions per request,
Far peaks floating in bluish air . . .
The other world. Anyone there?
"I talk to Bob every day"—yes,

Mother, I believe you, but does he hear?
What if there's no one to say hello
To the stranger, no banner, no band, no boat,
No shore. Blank as the lining of a mirror,

Its buried treasures long ago looted
And dispersed, untraceable. The place
Prepared in Our Father's Mansion, I hate
To say it, but never mind, my room

Back at the Hyatt is prepared, housekeeping
Has turned down the covers, the lights of the bridge
Float in the window above a dynastic
King-size bed . . . Good night. I sleep

Like the dead, and wake, to the harp-span
Of the strung bridge, its bronze rays
Echoing the feathered sparkle of the bay—
A great view, in the right hands,

Turner's for instance. On Hanging Day
He layers on more yellow and white
Until the vanishing point of the horizon
Rises, flowing toward us. Details

Of the bridge dissolve, and we enter a perfect
Place, where *son et lumière* exist
For their own sake. While over the abyss
A tugboat passes—updating Turner

Whose haulers and keelmen bend to their work
Close by a moon-drenched sea racing
Backward to its molten home: laborers
Stranded on the shore of the other world.

# The Eugenics Lab

---- ◆ ·

*It's only a "thinning process."*
    — "The Last Lessons, 1," Scripts for the
    Pageant, *The Changing Light at Sandover*

ALAS, JM, U WERE YR FATHER'S SON. THE SAVAGE STRAIN
OF NATURE-RED-IN-TOOTH-AND-CLAW DESCENDS IN CAPITAL
WHICH TAKES NO PRISONERS, THROUGH ROBBER BARON DNA,
GENE-POOL OF THOSE IDEAS U LIKE NABOKOV BELIEVED
U WERE UNVIOLATED BY. HIS DREAM-KINGDOM, BANISHED
FROM ITS ARBOR BY BOLSHEVIKS, LIVES AGAIN IN YR MASQUE
OF A COSMIC HIERARCHY, WHO WILL RESTORE THEIR COURT,
REPAIR THE RUINED GARDEN WHERE THE RABBLE PITCHED THEIR TENTS.
DOES THIS ROUGH PRÉCIS MAKE ONE GAG? IT LACKS THE MAZY ART
OF YOUR OPERA, WHOSE STAGECRAFT BY MARK MORRIS OUT OF
ROBERT WILSON SEEMS ANGELIC, BUT LISTEN, BACK ON EARTH

this note, "THE HOPE OF A RACE PERFECTED AND IMMORTAL,"
tolls a dull, familiar bell. For instance, though you wrote

"A PRESSURE NEW TO US HAS WE PRESUME
          TO DO WITH CERTAIN HIGHLY CLONED SCIENTIST SOULS
WHO FORCE BOUNDARIES AS YET IMPERMISSIBLE"

how new are these Promethean
          mad scientists we knew before
    in Gothic fiction, expressionist film

70

and comic books? And "real life."
           Speaking of which let me introduce
           *The Station for Experimental Evolution*

founded in 1904
           in Cold Spring Harbor
           by Charles Davenport

to bring the "science of eugenics"
           then barely named and still a study of
           plants and animals

into the human arena, adding a wing in 1911
           *The Eugenics Records Office*
           hiring the fierce Harry Laughlin

trained in cattle
           who would be the catalyst
           his agenda

"*sterilization*
           *of the feebleminded, insane,*
           *criminalistic, delinquent, wayward, and epileptic.*"

Major funding
           provided
           by Rockefeller and Carnegie

awards at county fairs with photo ops
           for "fittest families"
           to keep the country strong

prisoners sterilized
            based on his plan
      why be surprised

when the Nazis turned to him as source
            Heidelberg gave him
      an honorary degree

while Virginia
            sterilized "wayward boys and girls as a
      condition of release" and

called on the U.S. "to wield the pruning knife
            more vigorously"
      catch up with the Europeans

who'd stolen our ideas
            The Great Ideas
      which never leave us.

Prisoners plead for their lives
            kneeling in a savage sun
      in the dust

in the Kingdom of Kush
            4000 B.C.
      and die in their own blood.

You were right
            "greed and savagery
      are the tongues we've spoken since the beginning"

72

and "the great thinning" goes on,
        new foam in the many-headed tide
      breaking on the rocks

of Ellis Island then Long Island
        where Social Darwinism
      donned the white coat of Science, to answer

your call
        when you knocked on the board.
      Your method is Dante's but other sources

lurk in the heart
        of that song and dance
      echoes of guttural rants in *The Cantos*

and alas, *A Vision*, to speak of ranting
        here is Yeats (in his essay
      "On the Boiler," 1938)

"well-known specialists are convinced
        that the principal European nations
      are degenerating in body and in mind"

and "the Fascist countries know that civilization
        has reached a crisis
      and found their eloquence upon that knowledge."

Should we say that Yeats was spared
        a vision of the next phase—
      the solution shrouded in mist?

Wallace Stevens, third in my triptych,
          sat down one night in Hartford and wrote
     "the Italians have as much right

to take Ethiopia from the coons
          as the coons
     from the boa-constrictors."

What is to be said? I can tell you
          how Matisse transported his dancers
     to the walls of Mr. Barnes's house

in Pennsylvania, but not what became
          of Madame Matisse & *fille*
     after the Gestapo picked them up.

Reading "Sunday Morning"
          when I was twenty I thought
     a poem could change a life

but only privilege is altered
          by art.
     If not wealth at least the riches

of a physical world, in good health,
          and no terror.
     Simplicity itself.

Food. Housing. Work, though it leaves us
          so worn these words
     are of no interest.

# A Date with Sunset

On our way to see the chapel Matisse
Had called his masterpiece, we find a spray
Of flowers whose ribbons read CHER AMI

PIERRE, a local rock star, from the way
*Jeunes filles* step from their cars and toss their hair,
And kiss, darting into the gloomy cave

Of a village church. *Au revoir*, Pierre.
Undone at a young age by fast-lane life—
We're off, in search of the master's airy

Décor, which is worth the trip. Blue and white
Stations of the cross sketched on tiles, and robes
For a lucky priest: spritely new attire

For an angel without an aureole,
Elusive figure whose sightings are rare
As sun this week—a wet mistral has blown

In constantly, but next morning our prayers
Are answered: the mist clears, the Baie des Anges
Glitters all before us, framed by flaring

Palms which proclaim Valéry's message, *calme*,
The angel's bread and milk placed on the table.
This is good news for those *arrondissements*

Of Nice whose balcony railings are draped
With drying laundry and neo-Nazi
Posters for Le Pen—FRANCE POUR LES FRANÇAIS!

*Voilà*, when language dumps art for action
And the slogans of realpolitik,
Life is oversimplified. Such toxic

Waste on the Côte d'Azur shows how easily
The bad dream of a perfect race dissolves
Frontiers. It makes itself at home, even

Here, where Resistance heroes failed to solve
The soaring unemployment rate. No one's
In charge? Though only tourists, we resolve

To give it thought, but later. Day is done.
The seaside volta's in full swing, a crowd
Of figures who, backlit by setting sun,

Are half-abstract, like the opaque cutouts
Matisse made to float through Oceania's
Dreamy otherworld. When we turn around

And walk back east, we see the entire cast
Restored to life, old poets in berets
Ambling with their hands clasped behind their backs

While willowy girls and boys on skateboards
Swerve past them, and lean professional dudes
Pound by on a power run, their take-charge

Masks still in place. The in-line skaters loop
Through a slalom course at breakneck speed
Or set up a row of trash cans, to swoop

Across them, barely landing on their feet,
And add more obstacles, all to demand
A more refined technique, while farther east

We see the statue-mimes whose mise-en-scène
Is Galatea, posed on a chair, dressed
In leotard and tights, Pygmalion

Kneeling with his chisel. He looks depressed.
What's wrong? Is he worried that she won't spring
To life? or afraid that art *brevis est,*

That spell abandoning, after its fling
At metamorphosis, a girl whose heart-
Break lies ahead, marriage, divorce, raising

Ungrateful kids, and not a thing his art
Can do? It's a tough way to make a franc,
Which I drop in the hat. We turn and start

Back toward the dying light, the flame-barred bank
Of clouds where no one's home. No more waiting
For new books, no X-ray reader to thank

For divining one's better self. Your case
Is closed. Critics have your oeuvre complete,
A landscape of dead volcanoes, dry lakes,

Craters to name. What's left to us is speech
In which we know the world (unless we're doomed
Or is it predetermined to believe

*Words can only do for us what grooming*
*Does for apes),* in which we see the world more
Truly, but—how can this console, reduced

To your last words, over which I now pore:
*To see the other through* . . . the gates? . . . the mist?
. . . *the other free* . . . from the doubling mirror . . . ?

You're off the hook. No messages. No dizzy-
Ing virtuoso zooms through cloudy sky,
Refracting sea, no blue middle distance

Where you have gone, only a dark shining
In the mind where fronds of the bronze palm stir
Where the bird burdened with its splendor sings.

# Epilogue and Unraveling:
# Pig-Headed Father, Churlish Son

However, I admit that such a star-struck swoon, a dying fall,
Is far too easy, if the argument matters at all.
It leaves the world gasping with disbelief, as if
It were just what we say, no more than a mirrored globe
                                        spinning through the abyss—

                                        let me start again,
Less artfully. Your cards came winging back
With praise to feast on
                        and morsels of news
Like fanzine blurbs downloaded for admirers—

*Dear RH, I'm winding up (or my w/p is) the memoir*
*I began 20 months ago, and have begun*
*Teaching the w/p to write verse. Sinister how much easier*
*It makes things. All best—JM*

And now the posthumous memoir arrives, sifting gold from chaff,
The friends who called you Jimmy, from the rabble
Who knew you as Sandover's "semi-fictional JM."

I saw your star, from a great distance, as one to be followed,
If at all, with misgivings—
                        shouldn't one do something
That mattered, some praxis
Whose turnings on the lathe turned out
Bright scented shavings, yes, but more—
                                        a mace, a staff?

Or is it true, as someone claimed, "to live as a poet
Is the equivalent
                of a political statement"?

It's hopeful. I have hedged my bets,
Judging myself to be no worse than a bureaucrat
Of the Song Dynasty, those provincial governors
Who tried to rule as wisely as they could
                                        or at least
                                                    to prevent harm.
It is art
We remember them for, their scrolling landscapes
Rising into clouds, not local reforms

But whose life *does* hold up, worked over
By goons who straddle their chairs, holding cardboard cups of coffee,
                              glowering at the suspect?

Life reverts from gold to lead
In your recital of psychoanalysis, those precious chats which surely are
The hash of the leisure classes, no buried treasure there,
                and when a robber baron heir
                            whips up a poem called "Ginger Beef"
Art evades life
And life marches on, mocking art:

A late '90s item, this just in,
A film German soldiers made of themselves, some "pretending"
To be Nazis while others "play Jews," who pretend to be beaten,
And one wears a Hitler mustache, in case you don't get it,

Not the great winnowing, but the great leveling
Where we star in our homegrown follies, and skinheads film their rites
                to recruit for the Aryan Nation.

But when did our high priests ever matter
To those who lived outside the Lion Gate,
Living and dying indifferent to design
         the decorous deer, pacing in violet
                    around the wine cup?

                                        You have done
What you could, I have work still ahead,
A churlish son left to manage affairs of the island
                    from which your spirit fled

One day in Tucson when Della Robbia blue
Glazed the sky, when you entered the inner room
With "every last comfort," leaving your poems by the pool
High in the gated hills, where cars pause at the guardhouse
Before they ascend, to views
And market values more breathtaking at every turn

Above the city whose long streets roll
From half-baked foothill resorts
Through the molten center and out once more
To the raw edge of town and a technical school

Where semifictional Guthrie characters, Jesús and Maria,
Prepare for the service professions—better surely
Than welfare and armed robbery?—
A paycheck, a costume, a walk-on role in the café scene

         and farther south, where the road runs on
         into dust, the spines of the mountains rise
         like Mont St. Victoire in Cézanne's sky

whose "inmost depths of clear dark blue"
you plumbed, whose oblivious spheres are tuned
to a different scale, since you've been gone,

Since our sky—deep sigh—heard the last of you.
It's the wrong question, but, what have we proved?

Has anything been changed, if I mix in
Certain themes you airbrushed from the picture?

As if one believed that shimmering words
Could save a life. That art could change a world.

Enough. Among the angels, free from harm,
You are judged at last, and you are pardoned

For writing well. But where we live today,
No one has been pardoned. No one is saved.

# III

# Aubade Left Behind in San Diego Harbor

If a screen with its pictures gone into black, if a sneak-preview
Of oblivion, if that was it, when they carried you out of the party
Like a log, past the trailing sparks and the girls in their drop-dead
Black nothing dresses, their bare legs and the passing parade

Of canvasses rotting on their frames, then waking to this
Plush darkness, draped across air where the balcony ends,
As if to receive a dayglow print of aurora borealis or rainbow,
But so far this morning showing nothing, black on black, is perfect.

Out there to the south, behind the unseen sierras, a meteor
The size of a city-state, whose wide crater is now submerged
In the sea, collided once, and a cloud of obsidian-colored dust
Blossomed around the earth. It was dark. It was like

Being locked in a walk-in freezer by vengeful mobsters, and left there,
While plumes of snaking vapors coiled around you in the dark.
But today there's nothing to fear. The day will be fine,
Will be temperate and smug, as they say, and there, it begins,

With a flat line of electric red unrolling across the screen,
A hot flush spreading, a streak of take-no-prisoners red
Bleeding across the horizon like a cry in the dark, a rising voice
Pleading to be called a hundred new names, which you

With your taste for a siren song, are only too glad to provide.
Deep-throated dawn. Sticky-fingered dawn. To Do List
For today, sun-block, *Times*, bagel with cream cheese,
Iced tea with lemon, pocket dictionary, French or Italian,

Focus on phrasing, diction, tone. What else? A new approach,
Serious replies only please, no charming evasions,
No light-on-water rhapsodies, no science-babble.
It's light. Let's start over, with an easy-on-the-eyes idea

For openers, a blue Sheraton-logo S, traced in red,
On the top of a white shuttle van, circling the ring of palms
Down below. Off to the airport. Sigh. But what did you see
In her, really? Not the one with the brassy gold-filled rings,

The purple nails pasted on? Are you kidding me?
If your poem hangs on a pleasing phrase, Bashō warns,
Throw it away. This is severe advice. It can lead you astray,
To AA meetings, or to words that mime the mind's fitful flicker

Too well, to a blanched, bleached-out style where thought
Shows through like granite striations through a dim mist.
But you have no reason to fear austerity, not this morning,
At least not here, where the ridgeline melts, and molten iron

Pours through, pouring over the piled-up bodies of defenders
Who lie obedient to an antique esthetic, which moves us still,
Though brute brilliance is crashing through, a furious horde
Whose harsh disruptive barks sound new to us,

Whose glittering weapons, unseen before, will destroy us.
The rising clouds, soaked in that sanguine dye, discover
Deeps in themselves they hardly knew of, their vapors
Engorged with blood-rose and blood-orange, all her secrets,

Her stroked, splayed petals, floating up on display
To your gaze, which is all that they say it is and more, a mirror
Where her rising surprises, in repetitious exposures, rose.
The order of the day, however, is to find a new project,

Less flashy, less besotted, could we use a new biography
Of Maillol, to add to the annals of volume and mass, our latest
Arrival at the pool this morning reminds me of Maillol, her swells
Aspiring to persist in all that they do so well, in marble or in bronze.

She's writing in her journal, bent to the work like Saint Mark,
His bare muscular legs crossed and the bulky manuscript
Balanced on his lap, his head cocked as he scans for words
With a new directness, humble, and subdued by their message,

Untroubled by fear of failure or the wrong sort of success.
But she, as she writes, is thinking about her cheekbones
And how they tease out light, under the curved brim
Of her baseball hat. Is that the kind of writer to be?

Dear Diary. How do I really feel about this? It's all
So exciting and new! In San Diego, it's sunny and warm
And the same temperature all year round, something about
The ocean currents, well, "El Sol" is up and at it now

Like a sentry over the bustling harbor, as someone wrote,
Our second largest naval base, after Virginia Beach,
I did not know that, our dreamy ships lying at anchor,
Their gray shapes mellowed to absorb all scintillation,

To elude the spangs and pings of easy thrills, lying beside
Their dry docks without moving a muscle or batting an eyelash.
The soles of her bare feet flash, as she dives through
The thrashing surface. From below she can see surges of light

In tight repeating curls, and rubbery faces wavering down.
Could we see something plainer? That's all we have to show today.
But later on you may find that restraint comes more easily,
You give up trying to hit high C, the dinner invitations

Stop arriving, and the dim horizon speck is Flaubert's
Dreaded moment (to live, to have erections!) drifting your way.
And it may seem hard to remember then or care
Who was at the Palace, when you had to be there every night,

When the wild girls streamed down the aisles, to wrestle
With the beefy red-faced guards. Was that the whole show?
Today's sky is an open-for-business sky, in team-logo blue,
Chargers and Padres, with a high sun who knows what to do,

Who rises to set on Norman Main, in repeated remakes
Of *A Star Is Born*, while his wife is singing "A New Day"
And he swims out, sick of forever becoming a has-been,
Far enough—now, if he sees the horizon was not a trick

Of the light or another pretty face, if he hears the banal
Monosyllables of her song were just what he needed,
He was too drunk to notice, it will still be too late.
Are you fucking kidding? That's a tough crowd out there,

And the gangsters who crumpled hundred-dollar bills in the bell
Of his trumpet are not impressed. When you're talking to tough guys,
Get the last word in or they'll think you're whipped.
It's late. The restaurants are closed. But room service

Can send you bathtubs of domestic and imported beer and light-
On-fountain displays and lip-synch artists and the Snake Goddess
Of Knossos, whose waist is wrapped in gold, whose globed breasts
Float up to the gods—call now, avoid disappointment.

## Eppur, si muove

*and yet, it moves:*
            Galileo's

apocryphal afterthought, after having signed
               whatever was called for,
                        under duress,

the statements drifting away from sense
                    are you saying    I'm being fired
We have no choice we have to move on.
     Can we talk                about this?
                         The topic was Real or Faked
            could the photograph show
no more or less than what occurred?

               We stopped to pose that question and then
went on while the weather resumed
              the overcast and rain
      beginning our descent        into the area.

Was the Weather Channel the end of progress,
all abstractions all the time, satellite-photos
of the center of the known,
                  or a change in perspective.

      Was the photograph of the live burial
real or a propaganda fake?
              The exhibit:
These men of Nan King,
merchants, teachers, local officials
          distant heirs of the great meritocracy

*90*

rope wrapped around their straight-backed chairs
slanting into the fresh-dug soil
of the pit                    no expression

on the faces, that we can see,
           the print of poor quality,
                   smuggled out, its authenticity

                                    in doubt

their throats                  stopped with clods
cloud-stopped              estoppel.

Three thousand soldiers and servants    men women children and dogs
Were buried alive with Emperor Z.

Later the burials are no longer live, the retainers
killed then buried, and later, life-sized ceramic figures

                          each time believing their time was unique

when the questions were new, and the answer
                      meant what it said
                              when representation was real:

the chariot's ruined wheel,
              the mangled mesh of its spokes.

# Curious About the Crows?

A leading question posed in block
Capital letters, on cardboard, with black

Magic marker, taped to a lamppost
At the corner: CURIOUS ABOUT THE CROWS?

At a sound like a clash of palmetto fronds
In high wind, shoppers in the parking lot

Of Bread and Circus stop in their tracks
On the way back to their cars, and look

Up for the source: a ROOST.
When a roost is formed it may last

A hundred years, as the crows band
Together for company, for protection against

Predators and cold, against loneliness
And cold calls—the sign will not last

Long but as Balanchine would say,
The dance is now. From around the city

The crows arrive, rejoining friends or why
Not meet strangers in the night,

To share cozy moments with or
Even romance, maybe more,

Should take an interest in the sense of passing
Sounds, as long as their texts last.

# Eternal Weather at the Holiday Inn
# in Milledgeville

April and already steamy. Well, if it's like this now,
I wouldn't want to be here in summer, I say to the clerk.
He says, I guess not. His shirt sticks to his damp skin.
Reminds me of a movie I saw once, when I was a kid—

In those days, before the "feature presentation" began,
You had to sit through the shorts and the serial, where a white hunter
Was being pulled toward a boiling cauldron by pudgy "natives"
Sweating beneath their beige makeup, continued next week.

But I suppose the weather should matter less, if it's only a haze
Fuzzing the true idea that floats behind it. I'll tell you one thing,
It's hot enough for me. He says you haven't seen anything yet.
There is a thickness in the air and a slippery blur on the glass doors

To a poolside scene that seems to come from another time.
A chaise lounge of white plastic tubes. A pink bikini
From a beach-party film, the brimful flesh of Annette Funicello,
And what's she drinking in that plastic cup, dark brown with a cherry—

A Manhattan? It's a Fifties Revival, my high school decade,
The mutter of a young Marlon Brando and the arch croak
Of an *ancien* T. S. Eliot, and the rest of the mind's debris,
Indelible as the bright yellow plastic of a Tower Records bag,

Floating in the air, and caught on the bare limb of a tree.
Are period details another veil of distraction, or the real thing,
The plain facts that pursue us as if we owed them something,
As if we were in their debt, and the truth were right in front of our eyes,

Along this strip of highway, at the Dunkin' Donuts and the Denny's
And the Sir Muffler? Right across the road, they tell me, up behind
The meadow of overgrown grass, under the magnolias and chestnuts
Clouding the horizon, was where the writer lived, with her peacocks.

She ordered the first one from Texas, and when it came on the train,
She could see right away she had to have more. Now peacocks,
Worked in gold on a red and blue ground, were famous
In legend and myth, but hers were factual brutes, they were dirty,

They stood in her way when she came out the door, and they were hungry
All the time. Sometimes a peacock would lift his tail, and the screen
Would flash with illumination, where a thousand inhuman eyes
See how the weather will be, for ever and ever, and do not care.

Then it was over. One winter in the desert, visiting the studio
At Taliesin, where Frank Lloyd Wright roughed out designs
For what he believed was timeless, a rainbow rose from a canyon,
And rounded its radiant arch, and came down where we stood.

We gawked. What can you do but ooh and ah, if spirits of the deep
Rise up before you, converting their heat to a cool shimmer of ripples,
And vanish, without a trace of proof, a case of show don't tell.
If a synapse called on the blood to rise, and the feathers rose,

It was glorious, and she said so, when the telephone lineman came
And she had to make small talk. What kind of bird is that?
It sure is ugly. You just wait and see! But nothing happened,
Or not that day, or not until after he had gone.

She didn't make up her characters, she said—just look around.
The other world didn't come to Georgia, it never left, it was here
The whole time as plain as your face. And here she is, wearing
The fishtail plastic glasses that would come into fashion

Decades later. She leans on her crutches, her "dread disease"
Having come in its own abiding time from the webbed trees
With their sweet stifling wisteria-scent, from the black shades
Of unshriven sins and the gongs of sourmash gloom—but *lupus* now,

What was that, if not a tragicomic genetic blip,
A chance malfunction of the warning systems, the very accident
Dogmas say there are none of? Under the tall trees
She looks like an innocent bystander, grinning at the Brownie camera.

She has no intention of explaining, and no complaint.
Behind her a shadowy figure moves from limb to limb,
Always there, on the horizon, like tomorrow's weather.
Like a black helicopter in a desperate coked-up daydream

Where the powers that be are intent on tracking you down, as the day
Heats up and you wipe sweat from your face and a shadow
Slips over the cars at the mall with implacable speed, whacking rotors,
Background garble, Peggy Lee Ricky Nelson Megadeath Madonna.

But not to be able to escape it, the ragged figure flitting from tree
To tree, its dark glow falling like dusk, the terrible speed
Of mercy—that was the point. She seems out of date,
And may have thought so herself, if the mystery was old as the hills

And her task was to watch, whenever it appeared, and show it,
The treetops falling away to show the sun, standing very red
At the edge of the farthest fields, while nearer the plowed fields
Curved and faded, his blue suit, wrong for the time of year,

Her plump upper arms gleaming with damp, their words like stones
Someone had dropped, and someone picked up. "Time flies," he said.
"I reckon you think you've been redeemed. Well, if you've
Been redeemed, I wouldn't want to be." The to and fro she could hear

In Colonnus—"Come sit with me and guard my darkness. So."
"If time can teach, that lesson I should know." —the king and his daughter,
Under the strangely green sky, whose winds will whirl him up
And out of sight, a mysterious vanishing, into the unknowable weather.

# Divining

A pair of herons take off, flying low
Along the waterway which parts
The golf course from the mall,

Parallel to ripples they leave and a word
In quavering fragments of red,
A text which may be read absent

The auteur, like a row of digital shapes
On a dark gallery wall, whose shifts
To evade authority are endless,

"The use of sticks to form figures
Of continuous or broken lines replacing
Divination with shells, bones, and fire

In the Chou, in the first millennium B.C."
The streetlights sliding over the cars,
The herons in flight, the wavering ripples

Whose flame- or blood-red message is reshaped
As SAFEWAY, restored to its bottom line, its premise,
Its fragmented promise of subject matter

Flashed to the weary souls
Making their long drives home, into the desert,
Through the abstract, expanding pattern of roads.

# Where Was Voo Doo When We Needed It

Eleuthera Island, Bahamas, 1648

1.

Of all the songs the words
                    the houses of rushes and leaves
and the scorched rings of their fires, of 20,000 souls, nothing,

            as if no one had been here believing
in whatever had failed to save them.

How easy it must have been to complete the sweep, a clean sweep
of the long horned-moon, narrow as the rind of a melon-slice
                                    no place to hide.


2.

Rounded up and driven down to the shore,
like the citizens of Melos. They were pig-headed, the Melians.

How could the envoy from Athens have been more clear?
"The strong do what they can, the weak, what they must"—
but posters appeared all over the island saying *Resist!*

Now, when we sing the songs of their solidarity, we weep.

Every male on the island.
The methods, the scenes, unrecorded,
only the completeness, the bottom line, the will
                            to see what had to be done.

3.

On Eleuthera everyone, men, women, children

searched out, hunted down, tumbled into the dark holds of ships.

Where were they? What was this?
It wasn't night if their nights were luminous,
not death if there were pictures of death.

"The Spanish Conquest"?
The names are corrected, the point of view shifts,
                                        it is all the same.

From *eleutheria*, Greek for *freedom*,
"The Eleutherian Adventurers" were English
splintered from a group of dissenters,
                        purest of the ideologically pure.

They didn't last long.
When the next wave of settlers arrived,
                        American slaves freed or escaped,
it was already empty again

as it had been, after the Arawaks had gone, 20,000 souls
on their way to work in the fisheries and mines
                                of empire,
a "labor force," dying of new diseases
                        by the time they got the idea.

4.

*There are your tax dollars at work*
                                    my English friend said
as we sailed past our fleet in San Diego bay,

gray, stealthy, state of the art,
some still mysterious under billowing plastic
as if an artist had veiled them
                                    in a vast labor of love, to no avail,
some with their naked steel oiled and ready, their radar locked in.

Better technology
                        is always the key to the next chapter,
machine guns over horses, mounted warriors
over men on foot, the new two-wheeled battle carts
that made the Assyrians the terror of the earth.

Tell me you haven't forgotten Churchill
and his thundering oration to the House of Commons
*the new world now must come to the rescue of the old?*

Or the Song empire whose scrolling songs
whose cloudy landscapes
                                    mean so much to us        who were so hopeless
at defense, so baffled, as they debated and debated
and built their winding, useless earthworks?

5.

*Arawak.* Who knows who they were, or the words
they spoke, or the trances and traces of spells
                                        drifting from the African shore.


GOD MADE THE BAHAMAS BEAUTIFUL
says a sign on the AME Zion Church.


And it is, yes, even now,
the jagged glass washed in from the yachts
                                        buried in smooth white sand.


How much more beautiful it must have been then, one fine morning
when someone climbed the ridged palm, to see through a spun crown of leaves


the unnamed thing
                                        a high-riding hull
of pine, mahogany, and oak deployed with skill,
the rearing prow, varnished and painted, the designs, the flags,
all to be learned, *ship, sail,* and *harbor,* still to be named,


as the ship turned
and sailed around to the other side, where a harbor would be found,


to see the sun striking
                        on the curved edge
of what would prove to be
steel, of the finest quality.

# Don't Try This at Home

1.

During the gunfight, a terrorist blows the door off the plane, and surely,
One thinks, now we will all be sucked out into the shrieking vacuum,
Hopes and dreams and flight attendants, low-fat pretzels and small bottles
Of nepenthe and paper napkins printed with messages, geared to the level
Of your traveling companion, and glossy mags with maps of flight routes,
Red and blue swirls like circuitry guides for beings of a higher order,
Which shouldn't be hard, good-bye to barn and byre and the sexy vixen
Who stirred the fire, *au revoir.* Dead, my lords and ladies! Why
Is it hard to grasp what "end of story" means? That you don't get to gaze
As if from a nearby star on scenes where your friends gather, looking more
    serious
Than they usually do, more thoughtful about their hair and what they're
    wearing,
Eyes cast down or lifted, as their lips part, how pensive, but no, this picture
Is part of what has been removed, along with the contents of the rooms
Into which you could now and then look, as long as you had the keys?

2.

In a characteristic Vuillard room, *Interior with Madame Hessel Sewing,*
Life has been sucked out, through a kind of airless attitude, and replaced
By another form of being, like ours but different. The way he does it is first
To empty the world of whatever was there, until he has a bare canvas,
    and then
Cover the walls with yellow linen, between Old Gold and Mustard, and hang
The windows with pleated curtains of billiard-table green. On the floor
A Persian rug, with gold and blue worked in crimson, and on the rug a teak
    table
Inlaid with a diamond pattern, and a couch upholstered in crushed rose
Where a litter of small pillows is strewn, in solids and stripes,
And off to the side, in a rocker, Madame Hessel, who's scarcely there,
Bent to her sewing, she seems a part of the pattern but such a small part
That if her figure were removed from the scene you would not notice
The change, an image of the world without you, and how much difference
You make, a preview, of the sort Vuillard knew how to arrange.

# Stranded on the Shore

A glaze over reddish gauze nets
of vineyards, an incident report regarding blue.

Crimes against persons decline,
against intellectual property, on the rise.

These paintings had little to do with the seashore we saw,
he told us, they were studies in the theory of color.

To raze the archways bearing false witness
against dissolution, a strong resolve

where sidelong slants at the end of the day
cast modeled shadows no longer, but fall through us.

A tremor passed through her as she let her robe fall.
Rapid sketches of clouds dissolve and recombine

as nets of sparrow-flocks outflung, as particles
break into view, shaping a useful message,

a Stoic manual of last resort.
We had seen the silvered statue-mime at the bar

long past sunset, looking ghastly,
as if he wouldn't last the night, but hadn't he

made the invisible process of thought
look real? As parachutists blown off course

in their spinning falls to the fairgrounds
are no cause to abandon our search.

# Dancing in the Dark

Night-vision down the long curve of sand
      glow-worm grisaille
as if through a lens flooding the scene with monochrome light
like thought relieved
   of all but the afterglow of its song and dance
        brightening the night.

     ·◆·

But daylight was what we came for
what everyone wanted, after the trade routes were erased,
the lavish sundrenched heat,
the letting go, the getting away from it all,
ludicrous motives working their spells
      in cool cabanas
in the clink and glint, in the murmurous shadows
where all you needed was a good watch and skin-tight skin.

     ·◆·

Inland it was different.
No good jobs, nowhere to sell the beans and the corn,
equipment out of date, and dark heat
      in cinder block walls,
sheets of shallow water
    pressed flat by a soundless glare.

     ·◆·

Out on the bluff the vagabond dog sleeps through the afternoon,
dark fur of a slow bellows soaking up sun.

The flashy crimson blare of hibiscus repeats
      its one-note tale of profusion.

At night it is hard to sleep, in the long pull of a silvery seduction.
One feels helpless.

(I believe in karma, a student said, if something bad happens here
it turns up somewhere else, don't you think?)

But who can trace it back or track it down,
the centuries before recorded centuries
of savagery, greed, barbaric hope, and the new outlines
of comic book countries drawn over brandy and cigars,

the black hearts
                of words once gorgeous, now brutally sharp,
as if we were the first to use them, to shock,
to punish, weighted with all the authority
                                of what we feel.

Imagine seeing the world freshly
                                as if one could be the first
to arrive, the first white man to step on this shore,
seeing with the stunned sight of a conquistador.

Each night the moon resumes its place
with a motion so practiced and smooth, how can you tell
                if it is cynical or weary or at ease with itself.

In this night-watch the beach is clean-swept and bare,
the acres of shattered glass from the golden yachts
pushed down into the sand and smoothed over.

.•.

The luminous gloom of night is the right time
                                    for making love.
The cliff-bank of hibiscus, by day a swatch of fuchsia
wound around the gloss
of a dancer's drawn-back hair, as she hammers her heel and
                                    claps out the arcane cadence,

by night, by moonlight, is a lacquer-shadow
that clots and dries to a black waxy glow
we slide across, as we turn and pause and cling to each other,
"waltzing in the wonder of why we're here"
                                    dancing in the dark.

.•.

# *Becalmed*, the Director's Cut

Our plane has already been de-iced

but sleet comes over the wings again like a coating of dust
on the wide leaves of a rubber plant—
leaves I vaguely remember seeing, somewhere,

pancake-thick crudely outlined leaves, a cartoon version of jungle,
something I saw in an overlong childhood afternoon
when the promised transparent vision failed to arrive.

*Well, tower has told us we're on indefinite hold—*
*looks like we'll be here for a while.*

An elemental distention, like the melting watches
out of date the minute they appeared,
like the torpor my parents warned me of, though what would they know
of Tahiti and syphilis and tropical rot?

More static-crackle.

*Folks, we need to get de-iced again*
*when they can get to us.*
                              Well, it will be too late.

The man with the attaché case open on his lap
stops working, and stares straight ahead. Starts to sweat.
Literal, comical beads of sweat
form on the back of his neck and roll down to his striped collar.
Where have I seen this before.

A junk-littered dream whose faces waver toward you
as you fall through a spinning vortex
whose predigital realization is clumsy, childish . . .

He is going to be late for the presentation
whose fever charts he was poring over.

Ah, but look, rescue is riding our way
on a hydraulic lift, his Poussin-blue one-piece jumpsuit
                                    outlined against the sodden gray,
crew-cut, cheekbones, the clean constructive look
of Soviet posters when the revolution was young and fresh,

the sharp granite chin of Steve Canyon, a '40s cartoon hero
recycled on '60s T-shirts:
*it's simple Steve, you just take your tanks and choppers*
*and get the fuck out of Vietnam.*

Thick spray pours over the wings
and the fuselage, and the windows, to seal us in thought.

It's quiet in here. What were you saying.
First dada, then something, abstraction, pop art,
something else, where are we now? Stalled out.

Cartoons have a lot of staying power though, they keep recurring,
crowds of extras gaping at the menaced horizon, where Godzilla looms up.

*But after the third or fourth really shitty review, you know,*
                                    *it's not so goddamned funny.*
Well, try being too late. Try never arriving.

Try being more serious. More grown up. Don't deal
in appearances all the time, another thing
                                    they warned you about.
But what if the appearance was the whole show, if what you saw
was what you got, and in the final shootout
repeating itself in the signature mirror scene,
we are not receding from a radiance we once could see,
but coming closer to the real?

*We are number one for takeoff now, if the flight attendants*
*will please take their seats.*

# Smoke Trail

1.

In the domed sky of a glass paperweight, you can see
The snowflakes, the house, as if the artifice of autobiography
Were clear, but what I recall from the wreckage that day

Was puzzling and opaque—it was a clump of ice
The color of frozen smoke, in the shape of a world—
If the surface was flat, after all, but with a half-globe

Underneath, where the wires and cables are compressed
In a tight mass, their live connections and their storied
Repeating cycles, buried, and impossible to trace.

This random ice-sculpture was less mysterious
Than it seemed, and had a past, banal as anyone's.
Its cast-off form was once a household word,

A bowl, that someone had been using the day before,
Someone at work, in what had been the kitchen,
Under its slanting roof at the back of the ruined house.

2.

Little was left to say what had been there—
Charred lines broken off in the middle,
Surfaces blistered and warped, gaps of raw air—

Little of the house and its objects, and of what remains
In memory now, even less, the odd detail,
A stone of frozen smoke, a device, a charm

Where the story uncurls, beginning with the smell
Of smoke, clinging in every fold of the borrowed clothing
We would wear for weeks to come, looking dwarfed and clownish,

Living in unfamiliar houses, as if we were now
The children of other parents, or urchins whose fates
Were being unsealed, who might not need to grow up at all,

Revisions of the tale, from the thick scent of burnt wood
Soaked to the bone, with dark water poured in all night,
Frozen in stiff, broken poses.

3.

The kitchen was still there, in a sense,
As the body is here after age has overcome it,
A smudged, crackled version, a poor souvenir

But enough to guess what its life was like or invent
Its history, a tracking shot through an arched doorway
Past racks of hanging copper and pewter

Into the high-ceilinged hall
Meet for feasting and the giving of gold rings, for listening
On multiple levels to messengers' reports,

For searching out the dissembled plots of scoundrels,
For ceremonies to honor the good and the true,
Heaping heavy awards on heroes,

The Great Hall, gone up in smoke, remembered now
In the plucking of songs, in the balance and yoking of sounds
And measures, in the framing and the repetitions.

4.

"I think I smell smoke"
Was the clear message I brought to my parents' room
To wake them. It was three in the morning.

We ran to the house across the street
And clustered inside, pressed to its front windows
Like musical-comedy waifs

In our pajamas, our faces glowing
As we watched the flames, under arcs of water
Playing across them, flare up, and fall,

And flare up again, variations and repetitions
Of an unrepeatable performance.
I must have been frightened, but what I recall

Is how intense the drama was, how heightened
The world became, as it did when circles of ice-blue light
Swept across a stage, igniting the dusty air.

5.

Because I had roused them, I was called the hero,
A role one could weigh in the hand with other models,
The boy who cried wolf, and the Spartan boy who was so tough

He wouldn't cry out when a fox was eating his stomach.
But I must have known even then
I didn't deserve it, if all I had done was show up.

If there was a hero, it was my father.
When the way to my brother's room was blocked by smoke
He ran out in his bare feet to break through the window,

Leaving a trail of blood on the snow.
It would be years before I knew all this,
Piecing it all together from what I had heard, and still more years

Before I could learn the emotions to fit the events,
And the postures of lament, among the figures
Arranged, cascading downward, for the deposition.

6.

I think of his terror, and what it must have been like.
Did I ever ask? I wanted to know what he felt,
Not a prescription for what to feel. Well,

What difference could it make now.
Some days a cluster of years will lift away and leave me
Looking at thin air, through a window streaked with dust,

At the brownstone canyon and the entrances across the street,
The gold lettering of 131 and 135, their granite pillars,
Their architrave painted Minoan red.

But I still come back to the question.
Did you cry out in panic, or was voice locked in your throat
As you ran around the house to rescue my brother,

Rushing us across the street, no time for clothes,
Shoes, bathrobes, as the neighbors' lights went on
And we went inside, and were all accounted for?

7.

Did you think it might have been your fault?
If you knew about the flaw in the furnace wall, the crack
In the chimney, or is this from an Ibsen play.

I wish I could have spared you that dread, and later, the pain
Of an alien son, a dour judge, and all our distance—
How much was my fault, or yours, who knows,

If it matters now, if it ever did. I would spare you
The thinly disguised fear of your last years,
Greeting the cancer with blustering shaman lore.

Saigyo was said to have cured a man with a poem.
I would have done so, surely, but I knew no charm
And I had no use for yours. It doesn't work, by the way.

Did you realize that? I hope not.
I can see you swallowing hard, in a last snapshot,
A thin smile in place of your stock-in-trade grin.

8.

Half a century later, if I look down
The long trestle table, in the gloom of the dark wainscoting,
At the brass sconce, at the globed decanter of air,

At the pewter bowl swirling a bouquet of light
And the piece of marble from Delphi, and the small dark icon
Where some anonymous saint gestures beneath a skeletal tree,

And the reed threshing basket, which on this wall
Is ornamental, among these objects one could live without,
At the far end of the room is a mirror, and someone

The age of Yeats when he called himself a scarecrow
And a "smiling public man." I was 20, in a long black coat
With the collar turned up, and a cigarette squint, in a grainy photo

At the rooftop café of the Modern Museum, I think.
But who is this aging public man, whose smile
In the latest portrait would make a father proud?

9.

An image of my father from before I remember him,
Found where you find these things, in an album
On a table, next to a doily and a glass paperweight:

It is a small, square, sepia snapshot.
He looks young to me, around thirty,
His foot on the car's bumper, elbow on his knee—

It is a pose, but one that comes naturally.
You could bask in the glow of his self-regard,
The nonchalance of seeing himself reflected

In our gaze: how sharp he looks in his 3 G's suit,
The sleeve fitted to the cuff of the shirt, the cuff to the wrist,
Like a dapper dandy in a Fitzgerald novel,

Like my son, these days, as he bestrides the city,
Walking to work in a blue pin-striped suit, the hero
Of the next chapter, the bard of the new saga.

10.

He is a lawyer now, and of the deep plunges
Of recovered memory and their inventions, he knows too much.
As to whether a certain object, dredged up, will yield

Its secrets, it all depends. Do you want to know
What it leads back to? Or plant it, for someone else to find.
Or bury it where it can't be discovered. Responsibility,

He says, is not a matter of what you have done
Or failed to do, or the guilt you feel, but only of what
Is admitted in evidence and put on display.

Remember, he coaches his clients, the less you know the better.
I can't be sure, I don't recall, those are the answers
He has them rehearse until they begin to believe them.

Until the alternate versions of their own histories,
Those deep sources of the possible, are sparks
Flickering out one by one, in stone-dense dark.

# In the Open

A stockade for Rebel prisoners, in the rolling hills
of New York, had a staircase outside the wall
ladies could climb, to see them, roasting or freezing,
and always starving, these elegant sons of the South
whose ululations had terrified.

      Frederick Olmsted
labored in that decade, to show us open spaces
as art. When your carriage rolled
into Shelburne Farms, the grounds unveiled their charms

like a stripper, as sculpted hills and cleared fields
hid themselves and peeked out again, down to the great house
on Lake Champlain.
      Shooting was all the rage—on a single day
the guests shot a thousand ducks, laid out in rows.

      From the coast of Maine
before legislation drove them offshore
you could see the Russian factory boats,
later the Japanese, and our own, their steel scours
raking the bottom so fiercely, they scraped it clean

       bare as Carthage
when the Romans plowed its stones under ground, concluding,
if they valued their way of life, then every oration ending
with *Carthage must fall*, was right.

Just lobsters and urchins now, and vistas, you can watch the mist
descend on the scene like a Christo curtain, and the island

detach itself as the tide goes out, a prow of rock
and dense pines, beached on the muddy floor
of an ocean that brimmed with riches.

                              In *The Miracle of the Loaves and Fishes*
bright round salvers piled with mackerel
are handed round by ladies in purple gowns, with lace fringes
revealing random flashes of flesh, with the high cones of their hair
wrapped in pearls.
                    Their bare shoulders and arms

repeat the meanders, the knolls and dells we see again
in "the great white City of the Dead,"
as Emily Dickinson called Mount Auburn—
an empty bog in Cambridge, until they saw its use—

                                        as the Spartans
could see an abandoned Sicilian quarry
was perfect, for Athenian prisoners—out in the open,
tormented in every weather, and starving,
while their guards looked down overhead.

Their faces gaunt, their beards matted,
they were hideous, these men who had been so beautiful,

so oiled and tuned, when the sight
of their long flowing hair, combed back and bound in ribbons,
as they marched in tight formations, struck fear
in their enemies' hearts.

# Moon Pie on the Hill

Revealed, at the top of the hill, is it safe
                                                                to talk here?
                A round white light
                                I know what it was
                                                                                No you know nothing
but if there is nothing left to know        we take comfort
in knowing how much was kept from us
                                                                in disclosing that

in our rants
                        at credit                capital
                                                at antique standards,

the Venetian ducat, the great round weight of it,
a standard for centuries                a sound basis

                        . . . for prison expansion?                yes!

sounding good tonight guys, fulminations        raves        slam dunks
women and children first/fuck them/is there time

the fix                is always in
all language        fixed
all prisons        political        all writing blocks                all        lacunae,

permanent lapses
                                        we have taken credit
for knowing he knew all along
though we couldn't prove it, for knowing
the plausible others
knew, while the air bubble rose in the brain
of the last credible witness
                                        and burst,

known and shredded, details
eroding

                              sweat shine on roughened skin    under
                                 the raked angle of his cap
                     the pock-marked surface    our guys

have landed

at the top of the hill, a disclosure      a luminous globe

        from the other world
                 is not what it used to be

high rewind hum             flashed back to vaults
                     to decay

your testimony a tissue of lies, no antic
                       too labyrinthine or grotesque
pursued through grottoes           behind it    down

byways      bayous
            of local color    backtracks    crashes    twang.

The hilltop vision of a moon whose fullness
was hard to believe    marmoreal gleam
      of an unfragmented thought
                  Praxitelian

                     figures

along the colonnade, the ghosts of authority.

Do we still take credit

                for having defaced them.

# Shot on Site

*Boca Raton Poolside*

    Ankle-chain, tattoo on her calf,
butterfly? Or bat?
    Zoom in on that.

*Art versus Life at a Nevada Truck Stop*

    Arc-lights slant on black:
Ed Ruscha's bold ink-blocks, bright clean lines,
    All night long.

*Bad Night on the New Road near Sierra Vista*

    Dogs bark,
Tall storm clouds pile up, darkness falls fast
    Over Desert Storm Road.

*Race Point, Cape Cod*

    Girl fly-casting, backswing, fling,
Deep heel-prints in sand,
    Her T-shirt rides up.

*Island of Hoy, Orkneys, near Peter Maxwell Davies's House*

    An austere composer
Could bear to hear
    These bare cliff winds, these sea-moans.

*Running over Something along the San Pedro*

    Moon-curve, evening star,
High desert sky, staring up.
      A thump. What was that?

·•·

*Descending through Levels of Phoenix*

    Heavenly blue dome.
Floating white smog-veil.
      Sky Harbor Airport. Drive home.

·•·

*Moving Walkways under Montparnasse*

    Readers, books on rail,
Short skirts, bare legs, baguettes, pass by,
      Vibratory.

·•·

*Cold Morning in the Peleponnesus*

    Shade of the plane-tree, a dark priest
Pulls the bell, blows on coals,
      No one comes.

·•·

*Tombstone, Arizona*

    Wide raw street. Apaches gone.
Germans in Stetsons and boots.
      All dead shots.

·•·

126

*At a Gas Station near the Mexican Border*

    Pack of Camels, jumps back
In her truck—light-flick, eye-flash,
    Reverses—wait!

·✦·

*Hirschorn Sculpture Garden after Hours*

    Night falls.
Grand gestures, heroic shoulders, Maillol's tits & ass
    Dissolve.

·✦·

# Phony Winter Solstice
# Ceremonies Unmasked

### 1.

The approach is brutal though one can miss
The day itself, as in the onset of mind-loss,

There is less and less,
And one afternoon a sense

Of something missing, a darkness
Filling the air like depression

Without the indulgence, the grievance,
The plea for a parent you don't deserve.


### 2.

When the day arrives
They say it doesn't get worse than this.
They are lying but you knew that.

Experience is the great teacher, they say,
And they aren't all wrong.
The nights are long for a long time,

The bleak days brief,
A certain relief in this,
Less temptation, less nostalgia

For styles humiliated now,
A playing of fingers through glossy hair,
A lifting of hands, to gesture.

3.

If you miss the day
If you forget

To walk deeply into the woods
Setting prints of observance in the snow,

You haven't missed much.
The night was dark, and the morning

A reprise of night-shapes
As snow with cracked designs

And light like a grudging admission
Someone was right all along,

Expressions with little to add
But their lack of pretense.


4.

Is this a time for the mind to be stony,
Or to hope that ambivalence
Will return to favor?

A ski mask over his face
Blotched with red and pock-marked,
The wretched smile that read as a smirk—

A coil of rope around his shoulder
Like a mountaineer or an acrobat
Equipped for a pointless feat—

There was so much darkness that night,
He couldn't be seen as he climbed
And dropped with an inrush of breath

Through a chute of snow-thickened air.
The next day, no one could miss him.
No one could miss that plain statement.

# Spring Not Seen

*The spring we don't see—*
*on the back of a hand mirror*
*a plum tree in flower.*
*—Bashō*

In memoriam, Marcia Chesbrough, and for Ron

1.

*Discussing "The Spell of the Sensuous"*

Merlot glow, sunset, lake—
A loopy book—looking
For something to say.

2.

Tarot cards on your bed, divining
What can't be said ("She
Won't see spring").

3.

"Still make me laugh," you said.
Last call. Deep, echoing cough.
Laugh at what though.

4.

*Giving "The Widow's Lament in Springtime" to Ron*

Art's mirror held
To nature, clear of your last breath.
So? No help at all.

5.

Full moon. Wakes
In his half-full bed. Too early to get up.
Too late too.

6.

Apple trees, breeze.
Moony dowsers dip and bow.
Dance of the lost and found.

# John Ford on His Death Bed

If a single gesture can move us to tears, it is not
The effect of style, but because our reservoir of tears
Is full. At the end of Ford's great film *The Searchers*,
We see John Wayne in the doorway, an inside-out shot,

The low-roofed hacienda, from its dark interior
Out to the fierce desert sun. He looks back
As he turns to go, his elbow crooked and a hand
On his hip, in the signature pose of Harry Cary,

A movie cowboy, forgotten, though not by Wayne,
Or by Cary's widow, who bursts into tears at the sight.
Ford could have cared less—he had no style,
No theory—just point and shoot, he would say,

But a visitor, who paused outside the door, could see him
Making last-minute arrangements: caught in the act
Of shoving a blunt cigar in his mouth and leaning back
To look ironic, or iconic. In Kitaj's painting of the scene,

He's still gruff, but around him the queasy signs
Of hopeless symbolism have begun to appear,
A mirror like a window where antic shadows slither
Around a pole wreathed with popcorn strings

Of fairy lights—the surreal claptrap of delirium.
Styx Nix. A picture no one wants to see.
Ushers' yellow cones of light recede
Up the aisles, panned from the black interior

To the bright day, which is not hostile, but empty,
The sun-blasted sand and rock, the blank desert
Where Wayne drifts away, leaving him in tears,
Dying, with nothing in the works, and no theory.

# No Place Like Home

Centuries pass and no one passes through
The town, a famous stop on the great route

West. Not now. The motel is boarded up.
Gas stations. Pawn shops. Though a used book store

Seems odd. Inside it's chaos. Paperbacks
Of new age faith and deadly crime-sprees stacked

Beside dime novels and penny dreadfuls—
Junk, mostly, though there might be some treasures,

But why here? From behind his heaped ashtray
And smudged ledgers—a fanatic?—he waves

The thought away: "Just helping my wife—I'm
Retired, Marines—it's *her* bright idea."

Hey, it's a great idea, though who reads
Anymore. Outside the street is empty,

Sun-shocked. Reptile-black shadows. Killers crouch
In sunken grease pits, aching to get out

of their time

of Kansas

of Council Grove.

The town lay near the river, a willow and cedar oasis
                                    for prairie schooners
a long file of bleached clouds along
                         the trace of trade
                                              heading out

from Council Grove              the last stop    to retool and repair

axle, hub, spoke, and rim
                  back on the road
back in motion             as the rolling grass    closed over behind you

                                              Coronado

camped near the grove in 1540
                         amazed

          accounts of the time relying heavily on the same phrase
          in arias, at the top of each rise

                                   as far as the eye can see
                                         it was vast

                                         but it was not
the ecstatic
                         they came for,
with maps to complete      commissions         to finish,
they were traveling on business, we have their accounts

if not of the Cherokee, whose lands these were,
          whose accounts were burned in later      as policy
                  down the chain of command
                                   along the Santa Fe trail

                                        Kit Carson

exterminating brutes

                        clouds a mirror
                        of herds below, "we shot
                        as many as we wished"

from every hill it flowed away

                        over rock

over the limestone
                skull which was there
        before they were thought of, before
                there was thought

in flint outcrops

                                        in empty days
not yet known as empty
                        or as days

no clouds        a pure    infusion of light.
no word                     and no one
                                to say it to     or to see

how high the sun      how dark
                they are, in profile,       the pterodactyls

                taking long views        down    to their prey

feeling no awe       or wish
        for release                no rage      only this

attention and descent
        in off-beat        pauses      pulses      dust-stir and wing-soar
                from the cliff-edge

                                        *137*

                                        sail shadows rushing up
on the inland sea        on its dried floor
            ripples incised in stone, crosshatched eras
                                        to be named later

of intrusions folding layers
                back on themselves, into risen hills
silted with dust and        coated
                                with flowing grass
                                        as far as the eye could see

In what would be home, for ten thousand years,
To the Mound Builders and Forest Dwellers

And eight tribes including the Kansa, the name
Placed on a map by Marquette, to claim it

For France—a wilderness, crossed by Vial
On what would become The Santa Fe Trail—

*Kansas.* "Bleeding Kansas," in the dark days
Of the 1850s, when Pro-Slavers

Burned the town of Lawrence, whereon John Brown
Knelt by the Pottawatomie and found

Vengeance was his, in the name of the Lord,
Killing two sons of James Doyle with a sword,

Then Doyle, with a pistol, at point-blank range,
A bright, deafening roar of revelation.